Lulu Publishing

All illustrations by Cameron May
Graphic Design by Jen Little
Editing by Sally Jennings
Back cover photo by Wayne Barraclough
Website: www.trefor.ca

ISBN 978-1-4357-1227-0

First printing 2008

Printed in the United States of America

For Gary, Jackie, Bobby & Amie

Thank you for your support!

Happy Reading

Kim Perkins

for

Anthony Perkins

My Rock

Many thanks to:
Cameron May, Sally Jennings, Jen Little,
Sharon de Boer, Kaitlyn de Boer, The Murray Clan,
Mom and Dad Barraclough, Mum and Dad Perkins,
Rhiannon Perkins, John Gillis, Sarah Perkins, Cindy
McFeeters, Bernadette Mitchell, Loretta Letendre
and countless others who listened, read, and
most importantly believed.

www.trefor.ca

What is Trefor?

Trefor Granite is a type of rock often used to make curling stones. It comes from Wales.
Trefor is also the name of the main character in this story. His name is pronounced "Trevor."

Table of Contents

Trefor's Home

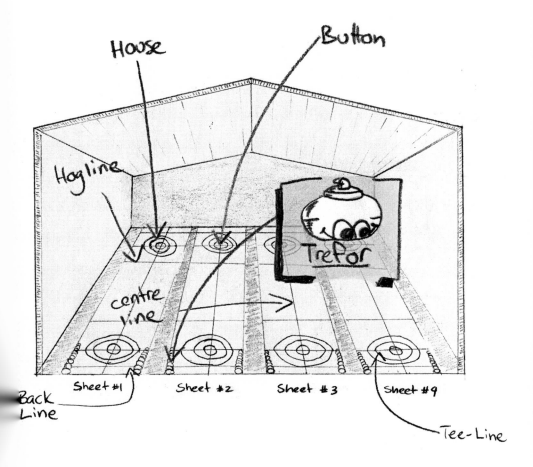

Trefor lived in a small curling club on sheet number two
with his Mom, Dad and five brothers and sisters. His Aunt
and Uncle's family also shared the sheet.

"I wish and I wonder about things I can't see,
I long for adventure to know what else I could be."

The Adventures of Trefor the Curling Ro

Chapter 1
This Rock Needs to Roll

Not too long ago and not too far away, there lived a young curling rock named Trefor. He was round and polished and had a handle on his head. He glistened under the bright lights of the sports arena. Trefor lived in a small curling club on sheet number two with his Mom, Dad and five brothers and sisters. His Aunt and Uncle's family also shared the sheet.

The two families spent hours playing together, sliding up and down the ice. Trefor's family would play games against his Aunt and Uncle's family. His family was the blue team and his Aunt and Uncle's family was the red team.

Trefor would often sing to himself as he slid down the ice. It went like this.

"Dooooooown the ice I go,
Down the ice I go,
Too and fro,
Down the ice I go!"

The song made him happy and he always seemed to end up in the perfect spot when he sang the song just right.

Trefor loved to play curling but sometimes he wondered what was beyond the walls of the curling club and if there were other games to play. At night, he would sneak over to the doors that led outside. He would stare through the crack between the doors and whisper in a quiet voice:

"I wish and I wonder
About things I can't see,
I long for adventure
To know what else I could be.
Am I simply a rock
Destined only to curl?
I know there's more out there,
I want to see the world,"

He asked his family and cousins, "What do you think is outside? Do you think there are other games we could play?"

They always gave him the same answer, "No, we don't want to try other games. We love curling. It's just what we do."

The Adventures of Trefor the Curling R

When Trefor pressed for better answers, his mother told him that she had once been outside when she was a little girl.

"Wow! What happened? Was it really cool?" asked Trefor.

"No! It was terrible, Trefor, just terrible. I saw a whole field of small rocks but they weren't round and smooth like we are. They were jagged and broken and had no personality. You must never go outside, Trefor. I don't know what I'd do if I ever lost you."

His Mom's story scared Trefor but he was still curious. One day when the ice was being cleaned and all the rocks were sitting in a corner together, Trefor was talking to his cousin Alan from sheet number four.

"Have you ever heard of any games other than curling? What do rocks play when they're not in a curling club?" asked Trefor.

"Shhh," whispered Alan. "The others don't like to talk about the outside." He winked at Trefor and leaned in close. "I once heard about a game called tennis. You get to fly through the air over a bunch of string!"

"Wow" said Trefor, "I'd sure like to try that!"

"I also heard about a game called hockey," said Alan. "It's played on ice like curling but you get to go real fast."

"Gosh," Trefor gasped. "I'd like to try that too. What else have you heard of?"

"Well, I'm not sure if this is true, but I once heard that when ice melts, it turns to water and you can float in it," said Alan. "No way!" Trefor exclaimed. "I have to try these things. I'm going on an adventure."

"Don't be silly, Trefor. Your Mom and Dad would never let you go. Besides, they can't play curling if there are only seven of them, and you've heard the story about the small jagged rocks with no personality. What happens if you get crushed up and turned into one of them?" said Alan.

"I don't really think that's true," said Trefor shrugging his handle. "Mom was just trying to scare me. I'm not going to tell them I'm leaving, and you'd better not either. Besides, I'll only be gone for a day. Do you want to come with me?"

"Oh no, I never want to leave here. I love my family and the game we play. I guess I won't tell if you promise to come back."

"You've got a deal," said Trefor. "I'm going to leave tonight once it's dark."

Soon the ice was clean and Trefor and his family were back on sheet number two.

"Good night Trefor, we love you," said Mom and Dad, kissing him on either cheek and handing him his favourite ice chip to snuggle with.

"Good night Mom and Dad, I love you too," said Trefor as he pretended to drift off to sleep.

He realized with horror that he was sitting in a field of broken rocks. They were small and jagged just as his mother had said.

Chapter 2
Off to a Rocky Start

When Trefor was sure everyone was snoring soundly, he crept out the door of the curling club. He took his favourite ice chip for company.

Once outside, Trefor gasped. He had never seen the stars before and they twinkled in the clear night sky as brightly as the lights in the curling club.

He walked for a while but grew tired because the ground was so rough. He decided to rest. He curled up under the stars with his favourite ice chip and was soon fast asleep.

Trefor awoke with the feeling that something was poking his belly. He yawned and slowly opened his eyes. He realized with horror that he was sitting in a field of broken rocks. They were small and jagged just as his mother had said.

"Hi, I'm Trefor. I'm a curling rock," he said nervously, but none of the rocks moved or looked at him.

Trefor looked around frantically for his ice chip. He wanted desperately to leave.

"Has anybody seen my ice chip?" he asked the silent rocks. There was no answer.

Then Trefor saw something glinting in the sun next to him. It was a tiny fragment of his ice chip with water all around it. "Noooooo!" wailed Trefor. "They've turned my ice chip into one of them."

Tears stung Trefor's eyes. "I've had that ice chip since I was a baby! What will I do without it? Maybe I should just go home before I become their next victim."

Her racket suddenly swatted him on the rear and he was launched forward, but he didn't soar like Percival.

Chapter 3
Rock + Net + Racket = Disaster

Before Trefor could begin running back to the curling club, he looked up and saw a yellow streak heading straight toward him. He tried to move out of the way but it was too late. He heard a "ponk" and the yellow ball bounced off his side.

"Ouch!" he exclaimed.

The yellow ball landed and rolled closer to him. "Who and what are you?" asked the ball.

"I'm Trefor. I'm a curling rock. Who and what are you?" asked Trefor tentatively.

"My name's Percival and I'm a tennis ball," Percival said proudly.

"Hey, I've heard of tennis before. Isn't that the game where you fly over a bunch of string?" asked Trefor, brightening up despite the loss of his ice chip.

"Sort of," said Percival. "The bunch of string is called a net and you get help flying from a racket. You also have to stay on the court – that's the flat hard area with the white line around it that has the net in the middle. Get it?"

"I think so," said Trefor, "but who holds the racket?"

"Kerry and Sherry do. They're over there on the tennis court. Do you want me to ask them if you can play?"

Trefor looked over to see two identical girls with dark brown hair. They were standing on a flat surface away from the field of broken rocks.

"Oh yes please, but is it safe? These rocks just turned my favourite ice chip into one of them." said Trefor.

"Yes, it's perfectly safe. Your ice chip probably just melted in the heat. These rocks don't talk. They also don't have the power to turn other things into what they are. Now let's see if we can play some tennis."

Percival whistled at the girls through his teeth and said, "Kerry, Sherry, come meet Trefor. He wants to be a tennis ball like me. Should we give it a go?"

The Adventures of Trefor the Curling Ro

"He looks a little too heavy," said Kerry.

"I don't think it'll work," added Sherry.

"I'm sure once you whack him with the racket he'll fly just fine. Come on girls, you were just saying how bored you are with tennis. This'll spice things up!" said Percival.

"Yeah," added Trefor. "I really want to try. It'll be fun!"

"Oh, all right," said Sherry and Kerry in unison.

"Why don't you watch me first," said Percival. "It'll give you an idea of how tennis works."

Percival rolled over to the court with the net in the middle. Kerry's racket launched him into the air and he soared gracefully over the net.

"Woo hoo!" cried Percival. "You're going to love this, Trefor." With that, Percival was paddled back over the net by Sherry, bounced once, and was paddled back again by Kerry.

Trefor made his way over to the tennis court. "I'm ready to try tennis," he said eagerly. "I can't wait."

Trefor heard Sherry grunt as he was hoisted into the air. Her racket suddenly swatted him on the rear and he was launched forward, but he didn't soar like Percival.

He lost altitude quickly and headed straight for the net!

"Riiiiiiip," went the net as Trefor tore through it and landed hard on the court. He turned around slowly and saw Sherry's racket lying in a broken heap behind him. "Oh no," moaned Trefor. "What happened?"

Percival looked helplessly at Trefor, "I think you're just too heavy to fly over the net. Maybe tennis isn't the right sport for you. If you go up the road a little way, you'll come to a swimming pool. You could try swimming but I bet you'll be a better diver."

Trefor was about to ask what a diver was but thought better of it. "I'm really sorry guys," he said. "I just wanted to try tennis. I didn't mean to wreck anything."

Sherry and Kerry came to stand with Percival, Sherry had tears in her eyes and was holding her broken racket, "It's OK, but I think you'd better just go before my Mom sees what you did to the net and my racket. Go and give diving a try. Good luck Trefor," said Sherry and Kerry nodded.

Percival, Kerry, and Sherry busied themselves fixing the net and attempting to mend the broken racket. Trefor sighed. He hadn't meant to wreck the racket and net. He just wanted to play tennis.

"Oh well, I guess I'll try my luck at diving," he said to himself.

He began to walk down the road towards the pool. He had to walk over more of the tiny broken rocks but he wasn't as scared as before. He knew they wouldn't hurt him. In fact, he almost felt sorry they didn't have a personality like him and fun games to play with a family. The thought reminded him of his own family and he grew sad.

"I miss my family," he sighed. "I guess I'll see them soon enough though, and I do want to try diving."

As he walked along, Trefor began to sing to cheer himself up.

> "Time for more adventure
> I'm off to the pool
> I can't wait to try diving
> It's going to be so cool.
> As soon as I get there
> I'll jump right in
> I'm ready and willing,
> I'm going to swim."

"Splish! Splink! Splosh! Glug!" went the water as Trefor skipped
across the surface three times before sinking straight to the bottom.

Chapter 4
Sink or Swim

Soon Trefor came to a building almost as large as the curling club. It smelled warm and humid. Trefor had to jump to reach the door handle but he eventually managed to get it open and push his way inside.

"Hey, what are you doing in here?" said a small blonde girl in a blue bathing suit. "Aren't you supposed to be in a curling club?"

"I'm from a curling club, but I want to play a different sport," said Trefor.

"What's your name?"

"I'm Samantha," said the girl. "Who are you?"

"My name's Trefor and I'm going to learn how to dive," said Trefor confidently.

"Hey that's great. I'm in a diving class. Maybe you can join my group. I'll just go and ask the coach," said Samantha before scampering off.

A few minutes later Samantha reappeared. "Come on Trefor, the coach said you could try today for free!"

"Whoopee!" said Trefor and followed her to a large blue pool.

"You must be Trefor. Samantha told me about you," said a tall skinny man wearing purple swim trunks. "My name is Jim, and I'm the diving coach."

Trefor smiled at Jim. "Nice to meet you. I can't wait to try diving. Can I try right now!"

"Slow down," said Jim. "I need to know how heavy you are first."

"I weighed 42 pounds when I was born and I haven't gained an ounce since. Curling is great exercise. Everybody at the tennis court said I'd be a really good diver," said Trefor.

"Oh, I think you'll do the diving part just fine," said Jim. "It's the rising to the surface part I'm worried about. Can you float?"

Samantha interrupted, "I weigh 60 pounds, and I float really well. I bet Trefor will too."

"What do you think, Trefor?" said Jim. "Have you ever had to float before?"

"Well, when people sweep in front of me in curling, I float along on a layer of water. Please Jim, I really want to try diving," pleaded Trefor.

"You're sure?" said Jim and Trefor nodded.

"All right but you have to watch Samantha first," said Jim.

Samantha walked to the long blue board that stuck out over the pool.

"That's the diving board," said Jim. "It's bouncy so you can jump higher before diving into the water. One of the most important things to remember is to hold your breath while you're under water."

"Sploooosh!" went the water as Samantha leapt off the diving board and dove neatly into the pool.

Soon she swam to the surface, gasping for a breath. She spluttered, "You've got to try this Trefor. It's super fun!"

"Do you think you're ready, Trefor? Or do you want to watch the other kids for a little while longer?" asked Jim.

"Nope, I'm ready," said Trefor and he headed off to the diving board.

He had a little trouble with the steps up to the board but once he was up, it reminded him of the curling club. The surface of the diving board was bumpy just like the ice at home and he liked the feel of it on his belly.

He inched his way to the end of the diving board and peered over the edge. It was a long way down.

"Come on Trefor, you can do it!" called the kids from the diving class.

Trefor decided it would be easier to take a run at the water with his eyes closed. He backed up the diving board slowly and carefully. He took a deep breath, and closed his eyes.

"Aaaaaahhhhhhh!" cried Trefor as he hurtled down the diving board, off the end and into the water.

"Splish! Splink! Splosh! Glug!" went the water as Trefor skipped across the surface three times before sinking straight to the bottom.

He hit the bottom with a dull thud and waited to begin the rise to the surface. Nothing happened.

He held his breath just as Jim had said, but he couldn't hold it much longer. His cheeks began to puff out and his eyes bulged. "I've got to get back to the surface," thought Trefor.

Suddenly, Trefor saw a long orange pole in front of him. He could see Jim standing on the edge of the pool holding the pole and miming for Trefor to grab on.

Trefor spun round so that the pole would hook his handle. Then Jim and the kids from the diving class began to heave him out of the water. Finally, he broke the surface and took a huge gulp of air.

Jim managed to drag him over to the edge of the pool. Trefor lay on his side, gasping.

"I don't think diving is the sport for me," said Trefor between gulps of air. "I wish I could find something I'm good at," he said with a sigh. "What am I going to do?"

"Have you ever tried hockey, Trefor?" asked Jim.

"No, but I've heard of it. Don't you play it on ice?" replied Trefor.

"Yeah, you play on ice and you get pushed around by people with sticks who try to get you into a net," answered Jim.

"A net like in tennis?" asked Trefor sceptically.

"It's similar," said Jim, "but not quite the same. There's a net at either end of the ice and you want to get in the net. In tennis, you want to go over the net."

"That was my problem in tennis," said Trefor. "I couldn't get over the net. Maybe I would be good at hockey. How do I get to the rink?"

"Well actually it's attached to the curling rink. It's on the other side of the building. Do you know how to get back there?" asked Jim.

"Oh yes," said Trefor, "I can find it. It was very nice to meet you Jim and you too, Samantha. I guess I'm off to try hockey."

"Goodbye, Trefor. Good luck!" cried the kids from the diving lesson.

"Make sure you tell them you want to be the puck," called out Jim.

Trefor walked out of the pool and into the warm daylight. He made his way back down the road and over the small silent rocks towards the curling club and hockey rink.

The Adventures of Trefor the Curling R...

He was tired and a little homesick, but determined to try hockey. As he walked, he began to sing to himself,

> "It's time for hockey,
> Time to get on the ice.
> I've missed the frost,
> It's going to feel so nice.
> I'm going to slip,
> Yes, I'm going to slide.
> I'm way ahead,
> I know how to glide."

Trefor began to cry harder and slowly inched his way off the flat surface of the hockey ice. Tears blinded his eyes as he left the ice.

Chapter 5
Sticks and Stones

"I think you're on the wrong side of the building," said a short girl wearing a helmet and padding.

"I am from the curling club, but I want to try hockey. I want to be the puck," explained Trefor.

"Oooh, that sounds fun," said the girl, "I'll just ask my team if we can have you in our practice." She tore off towards the ice.

Soon she was back. "The coach says we can play with you. Follow me!" said the girl.

Inside the arena, six hockey players and their coach surrounded Trefor.

The girl who had led him there said, "I'm Kaitlyn, and this is Claire, Gavin, Cohen, Natalie, Jason, and Coach Parsons."

"So, you want to be a hockey puck," said Coach Parsons. "Are you sure you're not too heavy? Do you mind being hit with a stick?"

"Are you kidding? I'm great on ice! I run into other rocks all the time. How different can it be?" said Trefor, with excitement in his voice.

"You're sure you don't mind being pushed with a stick?" asked Coach Parsons.

"Is that how I get into the net?" asked Trefor.

"That's right. The team will push you in the direction of the net and Natalie will try to keep you out of the net. Natalie is the goalie. That means she stops the puck from getting in the net because when the puck goes in, the other team scores points," said Coach Parsons.

"Oh," said Trefor, "I get it."

"In a real game there would be two teams and they'd try to score points against each other, just like in curling. Today is a practice though so we're just playing as a team. Do you want to try right away or would you like to speak to our regular hockey puck first for some advice?"

Trefor thought for a moment before he replied. He had decided not to waste any time before diving and it hadn't gone very well. "Yes, Coach Parsons, I'd like to speak to the puck, please."

Coach Parsons blew his whistle loudly and a round black disk slid over to the sideboards where the team was standing.

"Trefor, this is Bluster the Puck, Bluster meet Trefor the curling rock. Trefor wants to try being a puck. How would you like to give him a demonstration?" asked Coach Parsons.

"I'd love to, but first you have to get on the ice, Trefor. Come on!" said Bluster.

Trefor stepped cautiously onto the ice. He was nervous after the disasters of diving and tennis, but the ice felt deliciously cool underneath him. He hadn't realized how much he missed being chilled to the core. His cheeks reddened and he felt happy.

"Maybe hockey is the sport for me," he thought hopefully.

"Come on, Trefor, let's get warmed up," said Bluster. "Follow me to centre ice."

Bluster slid off towards the middle of the rink and Trefor tried to follow. The surface of the ice was flat and Trefor just couldn't seem to get moving.

"How do you guys move without pebble?" asked Trefor.

"What's pebble?" asked Bluster and the hockey team.

"Pebble is the bumpy stuff put on curling ice so that rocks like me can move easily. It's made from tiny drops of water," said Trefor.

"Oooh, I don't think that would work very well, Trefor. Our skates would trip if there were bumps all over the ice. Don't worry, we're going to use our sticks to help you move," said Kaitlyn.

"I'm here to help you, Trefor. Just do what I do," said Bluster.

"OK, let's try it," said Trefor.

Kaitlyn gently helped Trefor out to centre ice. The frost felt great underneath him and the cool air nipped his nose. "It sure feels good to be back on ice. I think I'm going to like this," said Trefor enthusiastically.

"OK Trefor, Gavin and Claire are going to demonstrate how to score a goal with Bluster, and Natalie will try to stop them. You can be the puck next," said Coach Parsons.

Trefor watched as Gavin skated up to Bluster. He gently used the edge of his stick to guide Bluster down the ice towards Claire. She tapped the ice with her stick in anticipation. Then Gavin brought his stick back in the air, swung it forward, and connected with Bluster's bottom. This sent him speeding towards Claire's waiting stick. She caught the pass, stopped Bluster, and swung her stick back in the air. Next, she brought it forward with lightening speed. She lifted a corner of Bluster and launched him straight past Natalie's outstretched glove and into the back of the net.

"She shoots, she scores!" cried Claire as she high-fived Gavin.

"Good work, guys," said Coach Parsons as he skated up. "Good try, Natalie. You almost had it. That was a pretty hard slap shot though."

"Are you ready to try, Trefor?" asked Coach Parsons.

"Sure," said Trefor, "but will it hurt?"

"Nah, it doesn't hurt," said Bluster. "It's pretty fast though."

"OK, let's have Cohen and Jason try and put Trefor past Natalie this time. Are you ready, Trefor?" asked Coach Parsons.

"I think so," said Trefor.

Jason skated over to Trefor, while Cohen skated off toward the net to wait for the pass. "OK Trefor, here goes," said Jason as he raised his stick behind Trefor.

"Crack," went the stick as it struck Trefor from behind.

"Yaaoww," cried Trefor, rubbing his bottom and barely moving forward an inch. "I thought you said it wouldn't hurt."

"Sorry Trefor, I didn't get lined up properly. Let's try again," said Jason.

"OK, but try to be gentle," Trefor sighed.

Jason wound up again and swung his stick forward. This time there was a loud "Snap," as Jason's stick connected with Trefor's rear. The stick broke into two pieces and Trefor yelled, "Ouch!"

"Oh no! My favourite hockey stick!" exclaimed Jason. "What did I do wrong, Coach Parsons?"

"It looked like a good shot to me," said Coach Parsons. "Is your arm OK? I knew it was a bad idea to play hockey with a curling rock."

Trefor sobbed as he rubbed at the spot where the stick had struck him. Nobody seemed to notice. The whole hockey team had gathered round Jason.

"My arm does hurt a little, but I'm mostly upset about my stick," said Jason.

"What about me?" said Trefor, "I think I'm hurt."

The team didn't even look at Trefor to find out if he was all right. They just went on talking about Jason's broken stick. Trefor began to cry harder and slowly inched his way off the flat surface of the hockey ice. Tears blinded his eyes as he left the ice.

"I'm not good at anything," bawled Trefor, as he headed for the door.

He burst through and leaned up against the other side, crying. "I just want to go home," he sniffed.

"Oh dear, I was so worried about you. I'm glad the small rocks didn't get you. Please don't leave again, son."

Chapter 6
House Sweet Home

"Trefor!" cried a familiar voice. "Where have you been? We've been so worried."

Trefor slowly opened his eyes and saw that he had stumbled through the wrong door. He was not outside. He was in the curling club, and the voice was his mother's.

"Mom!" Trefor cried. "It's so good to see you!"

"Where have you been, Trefor? We've missed you all day," she said, giving him a kiss and wiping away his tears. "Oh I'm glad you're safe."

"I'm sorry, Mom. I missed you too. I just wanted to see the outside for myself and try some new games. Being away made me realize how much I love my family and curling," said Trefor.

"Oh dear, I was so worried about you. I'm glad the small rocks didn't get you. Please don't leave again, son."

"Don't worry, Mom," replied Trefor. "I've had enough adventure to last me for a while."

"We're going to teach a curling class soon. Why don't you lead it?" suggested his mother.

"Are you sure I'm good enough?" asked Trefor. "I didn't do very well at the sports I tried today."

"I know you're good enough, Trefor. We all believe in you," said his mother.

 Trefor dried his eyes and said, "All right Mom." He followed her cautiously onto the ice the pebble felt wonderful on his belly and he breathed deeply, taking in the scent of frost.

"When a player isn't throwing, they have to sweep their team's rocks. Unless they're the Skip, they have to hold their broom out at the far end so the thrower has something to aim at."

Chapter 7
Ice Lessons

Trefor watched as the grade five class filed onto the ice. They shivered as they entered the chilly rink. Groups of them huddled together watching their breath hang in the air.

Trefor slid proudly over to where the kids were standing, "Hi, everyone! I'm Trefor the Curling Rock and I'm going to teach you all about curling today," he said enthusiastically.

"I live right here on sheet number two with my Mom, Dad, brothers and sisters. We're the Blue Team. My Aunt, Uncle and their kids also live with us on sheet number two. They're the Red Team. We need players like you to help us get down the ice."

"Two teams of four people will take turns throwing us rocks to the other end. You can't push us the whole way. You have to let go before the close hogline and let us glide the rest of the way. We have to cross the far hogline to be in play," said Trefor, trying to make his voice sound interesting.

"What's the hogline?" asked one of the kids.

"Good question," said Trefor. "The hogline is that thick line going across the sheet at either end. Does anyone know what the object of the game is?" A tall girl with blonde hair and braces raised her hand.

"We read that the object of the game is to get closest to the button, but I don't know where the button is," she said.

Trefor slid gracefully to sit in the smallest circle on the ice. It was located inside three larger circles that looked like a bulls-eye drawn on the ice. There was an identical set of circles at the far end of the ice.

"This is the button, and you're right, the more rocks your team has closest to the button, the more points you score," said Trefor. "The rest of the circles make up what is called the house. In order to score points you have to be in the house."

"Does anyone know what the four players on a team are called?" asked Trefor. He was excited. He was really teaching. Nobody from his family had corrected him or interrupted him.

The Adventures of Trefor the Curling R

The same blonde girl with braces raised her hand again, "The four players on a team are called the Lead, the Second, the Third, and the Fourth," she said.

"Very good," said Trefor, "except we call the fourth the Skip. Does anyone know who throws what and when?" he asked.

The same girl raised her hand again, but this time so did a short brown-haired boy wearing grey sweat pants and a black hoodie. Trefor pointed to him and nodded for him to answer.

"Each person on a team throws two rocks. They have to alternate throwing with the other team. The Lead throws the first two rocks, the Second throws the second two, the Third throws the third two, and the Skip throws the last two," said the boy with authority. "I know a lot about curling because I'm a junior curler."

"You must have a good instructor," said Trefor. "Your answers are all correct."

"Can you think of anything else the players have to do in a game to get us rocks where we're supposed to be?" asked Trefor.

"Sure," replied the boy. "When a player isn't throwing, they have to sweep their team's rocks. Unless they're the Skip, they have to hold their broom out at the far end so the thrower has something to aim at."

"Yes," said Trefor, "that's right. The friction created by sweeping the ice in front of the rock helps it go farther. Sweeping also keeps dirt out of the way. The Skip comes up with the team strategy – that's how they decide where the thrower should aim."

"Who tells the Skip where to aim if no one is holding the broom?" asked a red haired boy with glasses and freckles.

"Great question," replied Trefor. "The Third shows the skip where to aim by holding the broom. They trade spots."

"Once all 16 rocks have been thrown from one end to the other, the score is added up. Whoever has rocks closest to the button scores points. Only one team can score at a time. Once the score is declared, what's called an 'end' is finished and the rocks are moved back to the near corners. Another end going the other way begins. A game consists of eight ends." Trefor hoped he had explained it clearly.

"Now who wants to try curling?"

Everyone's enthusiasm seemed to grow with the prospect of getting on the ice. "Me! Me! Me!" cried the kids.

For the next hour, Trefor and the other rocks helped the kids get their balance and learn about the game of curling.

The Adventures of Trefor the Curling Ro

Eventually he slid over to help a girl who was struggling to get the heavy rocks all the way to other end of the ice. "You just need to push out a little harder," said Trefor.

"I'm trying," sighed the girl, "but I just don't think this is the sport for me. I'm much better at other sports."

"I understand," said Trefor. "At least you're trying new things. I'm not very good at a lot of other sports but it's the experience that counts. Take what you learned here about balance and precision and apply it to your other favourite sports."

Later that night once the kids had left and the lights were out, Trefor's Mom and Dad came to say good night. "We love you very much, Trefor, and we're proud of how well you taught today," said Mom.

"We just hope you'll be able to focus more on curling now that you've got the adventure bug out of your system," added Dad.

"I love you too, Mom and Dad, and I also love curling! Good night," said Trefor as they kissed him on the cheek.

Trefor lay awake thinking about all the friends he'd made and the things he'd tried that day. The experiences hadn't all been good, but he still hungered for more.

Once he was sure everyone was asleep, he crept off to look through the crack in the door and whispered softly:

"I wish and I wonder
About things I can't see,
I long for more adventure
To know what else I could be.
Am I simply a rock,
Destined only to curl?
I know there's more out there,
I want to see the world."

The Calgary Youth Curling Association (CYCA) is a non-profit organization dedicated to assisting and encouraging youth in the sport of curling.

The CYCA runs a Calgary area interclub youth curling league, holds camps and bonspiels, sponsors coaching certification, assists teams with financing for programs such as the National Training Centre, offers funding and programming to schools who wish to expose their students to curling, and promotes the sport of curling to youth in the Calgary area.

For more information about curling and curling programs please visit the following website: www.cyca.ca or contact the CYCA at: curl@cyca.ca or phone at (403) 238-2380.